"Thomas Woo

bathroom sex. *Toilet* is filled with the liquid writing of human fluids."

—**Kathy Acker**,

author of *My Mother: Demonology*

"Thomas Wooley's *Toilet* smacks of brilliance. His sinuous, newsy, mega-refined yet weirdly aggressive voice gave me an incredible rush."

—**Dennis Cooper**,

author of *The Sluts*

"Both cheery and cantankerous, the stories and rantings of *Toilet* are linked by a battery-acid tone and a smart, atomic energy. Thomas Woolley is a wholly engaging original, and injects his humor with equal parts horror and sad, eerie nostalgia."

—**Scott Heim**,

author of *Mysterious Skin*

To a Fantastic 2006 – yours with love, [illegible]

TOILET

TOILET

THOMAS WOOLLEY

suspect thoughts press
www.suspectthoughtspress.com

This book is a work of fiction. Names, characters, places, and incidents are either products of the author's imagination or are used fictitiously. Any resemblance to actual events, locales, or persons, either living or dead, is entirely coincidental.

Cover illustration and design by:
Shane Luitjens/Torquere Creative

Book design by:
Greg Wharton/Suspect Thoughts Press

First Suspect Thoughts Press Edition:
October 2005
10 9 8 7 6 5 4 3 2 1

Library of Congress
Cataloging-in-Publication Data

Woolley, Tom (Thomas Alan)
Toilet / by Tom Woolley.
p. cm.
ISBN-13: 978-0-9763411-2-3 (pbk.)
ISBN-10: 0-9763411-2-3 (pbk.)
1. Gay men--Fiction. 2. Young men--Fiction.
3. New York (N.Y.)--Fiction. I. Title.

PS3573.O683T65 2005
813'.6--dc22

2005019469

A different version of *Toilet* was first published in 1998 by illiterati, a division of Menace Publishing & Manufacture.

Suspect Thoughts Press
2215-R Market Street, #544
San Francisco, CA 94114-1612
www.suspectthoughtspress.com

In appreciation for their hard work and interest, a special thanks to Suspect Thoughts Press.

And to Martin Pousson for making it happen in the first place.

XXOO

If a gem falls into the mud it is still valuable. If dust ascends to heaven, it remains valueless.

—Saadi of Shiraz, *The Rose Garden*

CONTENTS

FOREWORD

I hate junkies.

I hate New York, sex work, queers, punks and wavers, AIDS, glory holes, vomit, performance artists, dead boyfriends, damaged childhoods, mental illness, meds, compulsive slutting, aggro fucking, shock value, transgression, dirt, piss, scat, booze, cigarettes, tattoos, ravaged nerves, and flinty coldness. Even my own.

Okay, that's not fair. I don't really hate those things. As much as I've partaken of them myself or exploited them in others, how could I? But I am over them when it comes to fiction. Way over them. Confessional, raunchy narratives of sordid lives and bleak beauty? Mmm, not so much. From the 1990s? Uh, yeah, no.

Sure, I've written plenty of that kind of stuff (and still do, some would argue), but I am putting my prejudices up front in order to give you a sense of how much Thomas Woolley's *Toilet* surprised me. These days, the last thing for which I'd expect to be writing an introduction is a collection of raw, first-person urban tales originally published in the 1990s. Hell, the damn thing was even originally blurbed by Dennis Cooper and Kathy Acker.

That's not to say that those two, or other writers of that era of queer fiction, sucked. I love many of them and much about those terminal years of the twentieth century. But eventually, throughout '90s alt-pop culture, from Queer Nation and urban primitives to grunge and club kids, too often attitude triumphed over substance. Wearied blankness was easier to affect than bloodied longing. A gloss of potty-mouthed cynicism and Grand Guignol–lite was not only cooler but also quicker to throw together than honest desire, fear, and vulnerability. All those junkies, all those serial killers, all that random sex. It got old. Then it got mainstreamed, seen today in the jester decadence of *Jack & Karen*, the milquetoast iconoclasm of Wes Anderson movies, the saucy cockring jokes on *SNL*, or homo-video titillation from Sigur Rós and Tatu.

Which is why we're more than fortunate to have a revised version published of Thomas Woolley's *Toilet.* Amped up with two new stories ("Piss Bottle" and "Citizen of Chaos"), *Toilet* is far from some nostalgic *I ♥ the Queer '90s.* The narrator in "Fuckoff.com" writes that he looks "at shock as armor in a life that is essentially one brutal offensive strike." Originally published in 1998, those words ring even truer in today's era of Bush II, Iraq II, and 9/11. Woolley's stories break through that state of shock. They are revitalizing rather than numbing. *Toilet* is an electro-paddle jolt to jump-start our current times. It's a punch to the gut, an insistent kiss, a shot in the arm to wake up, breathe deeply, and be inspired. Inspired to fight for the world you want.

Books like this are needed urgently. When Janet Jackson's Superbowl tit-flash sends the Federal Communications Commission into a tizzy, something's up. When some sixty-six television stations refuse to broadcast *Saving Private Ryan,* fer chrissakes, because it had naughty words—in a war movie!—things are bad. We're under attack. Again. Now more than ever, we need stories about piss-drinking and drug-taking. We need storytellers like Woolley, Rebecca Brown, and Henry Flesh. We need renegade presses like Suspect Thoughts, Clear Cut, and Soft Skull. When the homogay establishment sets priorities around the most regressive, uninspiring, and reactionary issues (marriage, military service, parenting, the church), it is all the more important to keep the fringe alive. We need to not merely document our realities, inject them into media narratives, and resist our own erasures, but we also need to clearly convey: fuck it, we're not going into Bush's second term kowtowing to some supposed red-state moral authority. Woolley writes, "The truly interesting show is happening somewhere else, played out in the darkest, hardest-to-see, and most uncomfortable part of the theater, for free." These stories take us to those parts of the theater, pull us away from the corporate sirens of a Disneyfied Times Square or wisecracking TV eunuchs.

We need stories such as these, suffused with searing honesty and raw emotion. In Woolley's "Life in Passing," a child's "innocent trust in a magnificent future" meets the harsh reality that coming out doesn't solve every problem in a shower of rainbow balloons and pink-triangle confetti. I'm sorry, *Queer Eye,* but things do *not* necessarily keep getting better. *Toilet* says so, and most importantly it's no empty gesture of defiance. You feel it. In "Citizen of Chaos," the narrator yearns for something seemingly extraordinary and unattainable: faith. He wishes for "a letting go, a trust that I will not be consumed before my time if I rested from battling and hating the Universe for its refusal to be controlled." It is through such honest desire—for faith, rest, love, sensation—that these stories convey not only hope, but also inspiration. Fear, passion, anxiety, and other fertile ooze of the human heart seep from between the lines. Their visceral potency, their smell and stick, are something no sitcom can capture. Their passion, fighting through the shock, gives hope that not only can we survive—surprising as survival may seem at times—but that we can survive with our senses, our feelings, and our true selves intact.

You see, I love transgressive–New York–alkie-junkie misfits. I'm just tired of fighting. But the beauty of a book like *Toilet* reminds you so acutely of why we have to keep fighting, and why literature is part of that. It is not nostalgia for a previous decade, but a welcome return to a long tradition of small presses struggling to unleash shocking, stunning, beautiful books that inspired running naked through the night, getting drunk, getting laid, and writing more books. Kathy Acker, Djuna Barnes, Jean Cocteau, Sam D'Allesandro, Jean Genet, Maurice Girodias, Essex Hemphill, High Risk, Heather Lewis, Re/Search, Semiotext(E), David Wojnarowicz, and many, many others did not fight through words merely to create space for endless reruns of *The Birdcage* on Bravo. Their lives and stories did not carve out a path for us to be content solely with *Hairspray* the musical and *The L Word.*

Toilet belongs in this same tradition, and it is of even more vital importance today than when it was originally published. These stories, these trips to the dark parts of the theater, will make you hungry. They will make you hurt; they will make you feel. They will help keep you alive, rather than lull you to sleep.

D. Travers Scott
Seattle, 2005

D. Travers Scott is the author of the acclaimed novels One of These Things Is Not Like the Other *and* Execution, Texas: 1987, *and has appeared everywhere from* Harper's *to* This American Life. *Currently he is pursuing a PhD in political communication.*

CAKE

I have a long history of clinical depression, and of suffering from auditory hallucinations. The voices say things like "ugly," "faggot," and "kill." I started taking some new antidepressants a few weeks ago after having been off the old ones for about seven months. It was not so much because I was depressed by hearing voices again (there is a separate medication for that anyway) but because I *expected* I was going to get depressed, and I have learned that expectation of depression is usually fulfilled with the arrival of depression. I thought I might need to be prepared—it's about my birthday. Traditionally, at least for me, that "special day" has not been much about cakes, hats, or those funny paper toot-toot blowers.

The exception, though, was last year. Still no funny hats, etc., but it was one of those landmark years. Those ages with either a five or a zero behind the first digit. The landmark ones, I mean, after, of course, sixteen or eighteen.

For days before my birthday last year, I was nearly high. Happier than I think I had been in quite a while. It was not so much the expectation that I might get some killer presents, but that I was going to be an age I never thought I would see. I was utterly astonished and pleased.

Since I was ten, I had believed with an ever-increasing certainty that I was not going to rack up many years on earth. My family is pockmarked with suicide and insanity. It is my legacy. Grandmother and aunt, both dead through overdoses; my mother is likely not far from joining them. Sometimes when I call her, she can't come to the phone because she has her head in the freezer. It's not that she is trying to suffocate herself to death, it's just that it is the only place small enough to give her peace. She might stay with her head in the freezer for as long as three hours.

On the actual day of my birth last year, I cried. I had made it past the age by which time I had expected, with faux psychic conviction, that I would be dead.

This was not going to be a landmark age, as last year's was; rather it would be just another 365-day turn of the universal dial. *This* year I started taking the antidepressant just a few weeks before my birthday. There weren't many side effects from this new antidepressant compared with some others I have taken over the years. The usual ones: Prozac (boring, overplayed, yuppie); Zoloft (makes it so you can't ejaculate). The skull-crushing headaches and massive abdominal cramping seemed minor in contrast. I mean, yes, I had a migraine for three days, but had I wanted to jack off or actually fuck some-one, I could have, and, of course, I could name the pill in conversation and not be embarrassed in the way Prozac users must be.

Besides the headaches and the cramps, there was one other side effect: a feeling of apathy. I guess, on a scale of feelings, apathy is like a ten, compared to existing within a vein-cutting suicidal fantasy, which is like a negative three. However, *this* had been a preparatory ingestion of medication. I was thinking I *might* get depressed; I wasn't vein-ripping bummed to start with. Therefore the apathy was less acceptable. Call it a four, maybe. Before taking the new medication, I was at least on a five. Five equaling "generally desiring to not be unhappy, but not likely to smile at things that people experiencing a seven or an eight would smile at." So I went off of the antidepressants.

Today, the day after my birthday, I decided that having stayed on them might have been a better idea. Someone might ask, "What did you do for your birthday?" I would answer, "I rode around in cabs all over Manhattan in the pouring rain being late for everything, involving myself with people who neither seemed to want to do the things I wanted to do or who, despite saying repeatedly that the day was all about me, forgot that I was even there."

It is mysterious how an evening or a day can be utterly shattered because there is an event associated with it. I think, had I not said, "It's my birthday!" it would have been a great day. Everyone would have been on time (but they weren't). Everyone would have enjoyed the show we went to (but they didn't). Everyone would have been able to relax (but they couldn't). Everyone would have strolled to the restaurant (but we ran). And then we would have eaten someplace we had been to before and liked (instead of a place that had a reputation for being "something"), no one would have overdosed at the table and slid to the floor before the entrée arrived (which happened), and the entire group of people would not have been forced to sing "Happy Birthday" in a "something" restaurant filled with anxious, stressed-out, and drug-poisoned patrons (which, actually did *not* happen because, before the entrées arrived, me and only one other person—my best friend—had the patience to withstand another second. The others all left or, you know, in the overdose case, were taken to the hospital).

There are a couple of things I am holding on to right this minute that are making me not return to the bottle of antidepressants after last night. One is that I take pains to make other people's birthdays good. Those people will therefore ultimately be guilty and punished because I will have selflessly orchestrated a beautiful and memorable birthday despite their having absolutely ruined mine. Which, you know, will make me a better person. The second thing is that, over the last year, as a gift to myself, I have saved enough cash, made entirely through legal means, to pay outright for a full back tattoo of the Virgin of Guadalupe. Something I have wanted for a long time which I believe will prove that I am tougher than most. It is all about proof for me.

So perhaps the day that commemorated my birth was retarded because, at the moment, my life is not, and you can't have everything. Or maybe it was retarded because my friends are. I am not sure. What I do know, though, is that despite having a past that, if captured in a child's crayon rendering, would be all black and red crayon smashed into cheap paper, and despite being an age that neither ends in a five or a zero, I have survived another birthday and have another year to do with what I want. To play, to work, to win. And next year, if there is someone to ask the question, "How old are you?" I will answer, "Older than Methuselah, but not quite over the hill."

I am so tired lately I wish I had the AIDS. Before there was the AIDS I wished I had a brain tumor. There were times when I maybe even prayed for one. I need the sympathy.

Not really.

What I need is a break, or a reason to live my life better, or a punishment for living my life so bad. I am glad I don't have the AIDS or some other things equally shitty, though, kind of, I wish I did.

I never knew anyone with a real brain tumor. Just bad hangovers or that totally stumped feeling that makes you think there must be a grapefruit in your head. Now, regarding the AIDS, I do know people who have that. Not really a lot until recently. I think I am too young to have gotten into the massive amounts of forty- and fifty-year-olds that have died already. Some guys I know have slept with those kinds of older men, but not often or then, you know, probably for money.

I know it is out there, is what I am saying, and somehow, though I know all these people with it, I just don't have it. One guy I know licked someone's ass one time and got fucked one time without a rubber and that was enough to get him infected.

I did a mathematical equation and came up with over three thousand tricks I had sex with in three years. It was not an academic effort to come to that number. Among them, there was no one I could specifically identify. What is that? More than one a day for sure. Then nights that included maybe up to five. Glory holes, back rooms, sex clubs, etc. And in all those three thousand, I never ever wore, or insisted any of them wear, a condom. Ever. I would usually stop the interaction if a rubber got pulled out. I wanted the cum. I wanted to work it out of them and keep it down in me. I thought maybe it would make a guy think I was something crazy, like special. You know, maybe even a person with a name.

I can pretty assuredly say that none of those guys remember much of me, except maybe that I am a good top, head-giver, whatever. Maybe they only remember the feeling. Some abstract, disembodied hole that gave pleasure.

At Harmony Video or The Unicorn, I would bring someone into a viewing booth when the attendant guy was busy washing someone else's load down the drain with bleach water and a mop. Lots of times I wouldn't even get hard. I would just end up giving the guy head and pretending it was hot for me too. After it was over, I would ask their name and mostly they would act shy like they were embarrassed of what just happened. Maybe they were.

Usually they would just talk like a huge woman and that would bust the butch mystique of the transaction.

I would want to talk, but it's a violation of some gay law to open your mouth for anything but a cock or to produce lubricating spit balls.

I do know this one guy, Larry, who met his lover, David, in a bathhouse. They have been together for thirty years now. Bathhouses were different then, I guess. You could have a name and people might even remember it. You could open your mouth and not just to dump the nasty sperm out of it. It was a better time in that way, but then, the AIDS came from that time in history, didn't it?

I want to support my community, stamp "gay money" all over my cash, and go do gay things, but there just aren't any gay things I can think of doing that seem like any fun. Rainbows? Triangles? At least you can cruise in a theater filled with fags, so even if the film is totally shitty maybe you can get a date for the ten bucks you had to drop.

I went and saw the movie *Stonewall*, the creative reenactment of the riot by the same name. Overall, despite it being a "gay" film, which I usually find unresolved and poorly executed, I did leave feeling good.

There was no AIDS in this film, which I was grateful for. There was also no AIDS in the last "gay" film I saw. It was a documentary about gays in WWII, therefore, unlikely to have many drag queens in it, hence, the theater was pretty much devoid of guys. I did see a certain famous one-time talk-show host there with her girlfriend, though since everyone knows she is a dyke and I was left with nothing new to tell anyone, that was worth only about four bucks. It's funny that gay films don't have the AIDS in them and that straight films about gays (*Philadelphia*, for example) do. I guess straights don't cruise in theaters, so they have to put miserable death in the movie to keep the audience interested.

Maybe if I had been fucking women all along, I wouldn't have the AIDS "out" and I would have to culture the tumor thing further. Back when I was getting started with sex, girls didn't get the AIDS, and I'd never really heard of married bisexual men. I guess that has all changed. I still haven't met, in person, a woman with the AIDS, though I have seen them portrayed in TV movies.

There are women in my neighborhood who have it. I just don't know them. At the Allerton Transient Hotel Annex, right next door to me, are housed SSI recipients who are infected with, or actually dying from, the AIDS. It is a requirement to get in there for housing. The guys over there I know, though the ones I was most friendly with are dead now. Tony and Pete. We used to sit together in front of the movie theater across the street planning how to hold up a bank real good.

I knew they had the AIDS, and they knew I knew because they lived in the Allerton. I thought maybe they would hate me because they were straight guys and even if it was some bizarre subversive chemical deal on the part of the government or monkeys from Africa that got it all started, it was pretty much the gays who are blamed for the AIDS now. I thought they would hate me 'cause, in a reductionist sort of way, I gave them the AIDS even though I personally do not have it.

It did not make a difference to me that they were sick. We shared needles anyway. That maybe was the bond that transcended sexual orientation. There just is no sex when you are high.

I wasn't sure when they died. An ambulance is pretty much stationed outside the Allerton around the clock, and every day there is a tossed-off, urine-stained mattress on the curb for pickup. It was probably some time in the winter. I didn't see them again after that.

I suppose my time will eventually come. It seems inevitable, when even the safest person can get the AIDS and die the next day. It makes me sad, though, to imagine my pee-soaked mattress lying on the curb for pickup and no one really taking notice except maybe to blanch at the smell. And I wonder if I will find it as much of a relief to finally get it as I imagine. I can't guess, though the answer is probably no.

THAT'S KARMA, BABY

What is the name of the hex that makes every restaurant experience terrible? Whatever it is, I have it. As far back as I can call up in my memory there's an endless parade of terrible dining events. Now that I think about it, if there is karma, it is probably that and not a hex. Though a hex is cooler because that isn't about you and what you did, but about some gypsy and that gypsy being all crazy and just traveling around in some freak carnival hexing indiscriminately. So, you know, you don't have to be responsible and that makes you a victim, so I prefer a hex, though, yeah, it's probably karma.

Me and Matt DeSalvo and Carrie Hendrix used to skip school and go to the salad bar at the Burger Country where my sister worked and load up on lots of dressing, beans, and noodles, and stuff. Then we would drive around Portland and throw dressing at rocker chicks who were sitting on bus benches near the mall. We hated rocker chicks because they hated us because we were new wave. For Portland, Oregon, at the time, being new wave was enough to be hated. Though we thought, of course, that we were punk not new wave but really, we were new wave.

Sometimes when my sister wasn't working at Burger Country and we wanted to throw food, we would go to the store and shoplift some onions or whatever wasn't being guarded. One time we got a whole package of Oreos—which was great because they flew like Frisbees—and had a very Chinese-vendetta-throwing-star feel to them because of the way you had to chuck them to make 'em fly right. I think the best day of our lives was driving up and down the strip near the mall where the rocker chicks hung out and successfully chucking an Oreo into the spinning back of a cement-mixing truck. We knew that the Oreo was going into the foundation of some building and that it would be there forever. It was a feeling, like, of immortality, and also a secret. We had compromised the quality of a building with an Oreo and only we knew it. Sometime maybe that building would collapse because that Oreo had been put in a crucial strut or suspension, and it would have been our doing.

Despite the dining hex or my karma, tonight I had what was a not-too-terrible dining thing with a friend. Mostly I have learned my lesson and just eat at home, though I am getting into that phase with my friends where they are wondering what the hell is wrong with me that I can never leave my little space, so I leave it just to get them off my back.

So, we went to dinner at Man Ray on 8th Avenue and, really, the food was good and the service was fast, despite the hostess apologizing in advance for how terribly slow it was going to be. Whatever.

I was surprised to get through so successfully and wanted, after, to just get home right away before I would, like, vomit possibly or have an allergic reaction. What I am saying is that something was supposed to happen that was bad and it didn't.

So I am on my way home and I am waiting at the corner to cross the street and this woman walks her little luggage pull-cart loaded with only one bag down the cripple ramp that good sidewalks have, and it falls over. She is like, maybe thirty so, you know, capable. So I go, "Wow," and she just stands there looking at me like I said "you are an idiot" and really all I said was "wow." Bummer, fell over, whatever. So she stands there and looks at me and I am waiting 'cause she looks like something is supposed to happen, but I can't figure out what, and then she goes, all real angry, "Yeah, *wow*."

She tries to right her bag and the little stewardess cart while sending me anger stares and I say, "It's not like I kicked it over," and she goes, "You could have been a gentleman and helped me." And I go, "That's New York, get used to it." Like I should help someone who, first of all, has one tiny carry-on and who, second, has an attitude. Fuck that. So she goes, "That's the problem with the world...no gentlemen."

It's not like I wouldn't or couldn't help, but I have recently learned this lesson about helping: if they don't ask for it, be careful about offering it.

Earlier today, on a packed subway train, I tried to make room for an elderly person who looked as if a seat would have been appreciated. So this person looks at me right in the face and goes, "I'm not sitting there. You stink like cigarettes." Uh huh. Let's see, I was on a packed train at rush hour, I was trying to be nice, I scooted over the people next to me, I made a human gesture, and I stink like a spent Marlboro? Is it a hex? A different one, but sort of the same? A nothing-good-can-happen hex? So I look at that person and I say, "I didn't want you to sit here anyway." I just moved my ass back and opened my book.

Last night I had to go to another restaurant. Two in two days is completely out of the norm for me. I do no more than two in two months if I can, but it was another "appease the forgotten friend" thing. I tried to choose a place that I had had a good experience in previously, as hard as that was. Of course, I didn't remember until after that the reason it was so good *before* was because I'd gotten really trashed on top-shelf liquor and someone else had paid the bill.

The prices had gone through the roof since my first visit, and the menu was half the size. I guess I have diner mentality: big menus, low prices are better. Also diners are fast as shit, and that makes them awesome despite the lighting and, of course, the food being rancid.

So we go to this restaurant on 7th Avenue in the low 20s, which happens to be owned by this guy who used to live so close to me that he would look in my window and watch me when I was having sex, not sly-watch either but really hang out the damn window full-on and gape. And even though he got a lot of free weenie show from me and despite my thinking it was going to be good 'cause I remembered it being good (but really I had just been drunk), my friend got raw beef when he ordered a medium-well burger. I mean out-of-the-package ground round. Raw, for real. Cold. And our waiter, who had slept with my dining partner at some point in the past, was all missy about having to serve us. And I just thought...you know... this is a small town, and if you're a big ol' whore you gotta deal with the fact that if you have nothing going for you but a long plump dick, you will someday have to serve all those tricks you turned. Well, our waiter wasn't dealing with that fact yet.

My dinner partner just pondered on that raw beef. Pondered and pondered about was it going to be worth it to even send it back because likely the whore waiter would just spit on it, and of course, because of the karma/hex I suffer it was all just ruined anyway.

But when he (the whore) swung back by, all sassy and ignoring us, I decided to flag him down. Nice, like, not aggressive. Just like "hey, hi...," though really at eleven dollars for a fucking hamburger I could have had a ranting lunatic seizure fit and that should have been okay.

I just go to the whore waiter, "He's HIV-positive. If he had accidentally eaten this, it could have killed him." He kind of took it away real slow and that was that. Also, it was supposed to be a bacon burger and it was missing the goddamned bacon. Whore.

So, what am I going to do? What am I *supposed* to do? Likely, I will have to wait for that Oreo-compromised building to fall in and crumple a few hundred people. At which point I can be a good Samaritan, leave my life behind, and selflessly go to the aid of the survivors so that the karma/hex will be reversed or removed. One damn Oreo in a cement mixer ten years ago and I am still paying. That is my life. Though now that I think of it, Carrie hasn't gotten off very easy either. She died of cancer and

Matt, well, he is still in Portland, and in a way that is worse than having old people, who always stink of something, tell you that you stink. Isn't that like a dog poop telling you that you smell like a cat poop? I don't know.

That is another hex I have. Not ever being able to know anything 'cause everything is just so damn wrong. Maybe it isn't a hex, but rather that I am just finally punk, and punks have shitty lives.

I wish Carrie were still alive so I could tell her I am finally punk for real, and we could have a good laugh about that and then while laughing, we would discover through a rapid-fire, spinning-camera, movie-montage moment of enlightenment and horror that we were, ourselves, standing in the Oreo building and it would cave in and crush us, just us two, and that would finally be the end of the Oreo hex.

Jonathan leaned forward to look between his legs. He wanted to see his asshole. Keeping the flowery summer-weight dress pulled up around his waist, while trying to maneuver the mass of his dick and balls, was making the whole thing a little difficult. He would not have attempted this were he not sitting on the toilet.

There was some physical impossibility he was trying to breach here. The more he tugged his dick and balls up and the more he leaned forward, the less he could see. Partly it was because, in order to get into the praying mantis position that one must assume to check out one's own asshole, the more one's hips must curl under to meet the gaze. At some point there just isn't any more pelvic swing. You can either meet your hole or you cannot. The other complicating factor was that his hole was really, really tiny. Tight, as they say, and covered with a mesh of hair that made it nearly indistinguishable from all the other hairy areas of the greater mass of his rump.

He relaxed the forward curve of his back, knowing that if he wanted to see his own hole he would have to, at some later date, just squat over a mirror. Neither having a mirror to take to the floor nor enough time right at the moment to locate one, he put his hand down toward the crack, placing one cheek as far to the side of the seat as possible to maximize the spread. The long red Lee nail tip he'd earlier glued over his own nail touched the hairs that masked his hole and parted them gently, breaking the basket weave his underwear and his few waking hours had created.

Lightly he pushed the nail tip into the hole. He sensed there was no poop in there. Had there been, he might not have attempted the exploration. Then again, maybe he might have anyway. Poop was just food but, you know, brown and weird.

He retracted the nail, viewed and sniffed it. He sat back and readjusted the dress that had shifted somewhat lower, took another tug on the grisly mass of his genitals, and sent his hand back down. Scratch, scratch. The hair had stayed parted and had gotten a little damp from an awkward upward splash of bowl water he had made with his hand. Good. Scratch. Jonathan closed his eyes and pulled his attention deep into his head. Out of the bathroom, away from his backache. The cock-and-balls mass gone. The dress and nails remaining.

He imagined she, Jonathan, was having a petite between-course tinkle in the restroom of whatever restaurant she happened to be in, on this, her first date with a man she was ending up liking. A blind date, but one that might just work out. Somehow, miraculously, it was not terrible. He had touched her leg and was acting familiar with her, but not in a psycho or stalker way. He had filled her glass with more wine, leaned in rather than away when she spoke. She was morbidly aware that her breath might stink like a smoker's, since she was one.

Maybe we will have sex, she thought as she peed. She had not had sex in a while. There was that one ugly guy with that dick that leaked all that disgusting precum. Small, too, and ugly, like a twisted pig's tail. You can never tell. *Sometimes the real tall, skinny ones have big dicks, but then again,* she thought, *sometimes all their flesh is in their frame and god leaves the meat outta the sausage.* Scratch.

Maybe she and her date could go back to her place after dinner. She had run her hands over her rattan couch and picked up a couple of fistfuls of loose tabby hair. The furniture would not look too furry, matted, or broken down if she kept the lights low. There were no tampon boxes on the back of the toilet. She hadn't drained all her liquor bottles yet, so she could offer him a drink to suckle while she went to the bedroom and slipped into her diaphragm and her Victoria's Secret. Or was the diaphragm Victoria's *true* secret? She giggled to herself there on the toilet. But...scratch.

It could just be chafing, she thought. The panties she was wearing were mostly nylon and that sometimes gave her a problem down there. But she knew it was more than that and her heart sank. She could *not* get fucked with a yeast infection. Could not let him see that seepage or worse, smell it. She scratched and scooped up some goo. Yeast infection for sure. Mad now, she yanked her panties down and off over her shoes, tossed them into the brass pail beside the sink just across from where she sat. She pulled a single square of toilet tissue from the roll, wiped off her long red Lee nail tip, dabbed at the chapped vaginal lips, dropped the paper into the water beneath her, flushed, stood, adjusted herself, and exited.

She thought to herself, as she made her way back toward her date, *I can just blow him. I'll give him a blow job so he'll think I am so into him that I don't care about me and that will make him not think about getting into my coochie.* She smiled at that. *Coochie.* Spic, sort of, but cute just the same. *Blow job, blow job,* she chanted in her head. She got closer to the area of the restaurant in which she and her date were seated. He was gone. Had left while she was peeing. The unpaid bill remained on the table.

"Is everything okay?" Jonathan heard the man yell from the living room. Jonathan realized the dick he had been mashing out of the way of his imaginary pussy was now hard. He beat the cock against his belly a few times, three, perhaps, then stood up. How long had he been in here? The dress caught on his boner and created a flowery summer-weight tent.

What was his name? Jonathan could no longer remember. His reverie had so absorbed him that whoever it was waiting for him had slipped his mind. Rob. Tom. John. He had thought it was the dress guy, the guy who liked to have Jonathan waiting for him, all made up, dainty, girlish. It was the crucifixion guy though. That was why Jonathan had made his dash to the can. Had to get the nails off. Had to get the dress off. Had to get his head together and reverse the whole plan.

Jonathan yelled back, "Yeah, still here."

The guy answered, "Uh, okay. Sorry."

Jonthan pulled the dress off over his head, rolled it into a ball, and shoved it under the sink. The nail tips had not been glued so well or with much pressure. They snapped off without difficulty. Biting the last thumb nail off and spitting it onto the floor, Jonathan opened the door of the bathroom and made his way, nude, toward the client in the living room.

> *Man:* If I were a slave and you were my Master, what would you do to me?
>
> *Jonathan:* I would crucify you.

The man moved toward the bed. Undressed and lay down on his

back. Jonathan, disgusted, impatient, rolled his eyes so far back in his head he could practically see out the window behind him. *Ready... set...go.*

> *Man:* Do you want to see me in a position like I am on the cross?
>
> *Jonathan:* Yeah, sure.

The man is stretched out on the bed, back pressed against the mattress. He is trying to keep his abdominal muscles tight, his chest flexed. Pretending to fight the gravity of the imaginary cross, wanting to be hot. Hot for Jonathan, though Jonathan couldn't care one way or the other, he is not into this scene in the way the man is.

Jonathan wonders how the man is able to breathe all flexed and held like that. After a moment's hesitation, Jonathan puts on his best aggressive face. The one that has worked in this scene before. *Sort of brooding,* he thinks. A mix of vintage Brando and a young Nicholson. The unpredictable nature of the combination face makes him look, Jonathan believes, controlled, determined, powerful. The man thinks Jonathan looks like a murderer and likes it.

Jonathan climbs horizontally across the man's vertical body, straddles him, and presses his knees firmly against the man's ribs. They push inwards. The man must work harder for each breath. The man's arms are outstretched, one to each side, palms up. And the toes of one foot are placed upon the top of the other. He is, for the moment, Jesus-ish. Jonathan inclines forward, drilling his thumbs into the fleshy palms of the man's hands, simulating, as best he can, the puncturing of skin, the metal that would attach the man's hands to the boards of the cross if there had actually been one. The man's cock blooms red, blood is pushed up the shaft to the big mushroom head. Jonathan can feel it beating against his ass and lower back with the man's increasing heart rate.

The man, whose head is slightly inclined to the right—a gaze upwards, beatific, The Passion—whispers to Jonathan some word like "please," or is it just an exhalation? Jonathan is not sure. Jonathan says, "I love you so much, I must kill you rather than let you go free." His timing is not always right, but Jonathan has judged correctly this time. It is explosive heat in the room, all darkness from the drawn shades. The man tries to raise his head to kiss. There is a tear in his eye, and then the ejaculate from his cock shoots straight up and across Jonathan's back.

Silence for a moment, then it is finished. Jonathan closes his eyes, exhales, then shuts his eyes a bit tighter. Slides to the side of the bed, off of the man, and firmly plants his feet on the floor.

Dear Anji,

I am still in therapy with that lady, even though I said I thought I might dump her. Looking for someone new and telling them the whole story from start to finish is just too hard. I think I would rather stay with a bad therapist than have to go through that. Tell me what is going on with you.

Love you,
J

I first met Anji in 1982. My family had just moved to Portland, Oregon, from California. It was not a move I was in favor of, though at the age of fifteen I had no power of veto. I have never fully come to understand why we moved at all. Vaguely I am aware that it might have had something to do with my father looking for better opportunities career-wise. In the '80s I guess there was still a chance for better opportunities, though the whole concept seems really '50s to me.

Mostly I hated Portland. That it has the highest teen suicide rate in the nation is no surprise to any teen who has lived there. It is very conservative, yet creatively masked as liberal. The forest-green Volvos and Birkenstocks, etc.

Whatever my father did in California is not what he ended up doing in Portland. He went from job to job. Not making very much money. We had to keep the heat low, even during winter, and the lights, with the exception of the one you needed to study or read by, could not be left on. That was how we scrimped. Utility bill maintenance. It did not occur to me until later that, had my father actually spent a portion of the money that he spent on liquor on paying those bills, we might not have been raised in darkness.

Anji was just a girl in school like any other girl. I did not notice her much or pay attention to whatever she was doing or whoever she hung out with. I guess because, like me, she wasn't doing anything or hanging out with anyone. She in her corner of the smoking square outside the rear exit to Jefferson High School and I in mine, blowing smoke into space.

Brian was the one who brought us together. Brian Reif. Brian had gone to Jefferson too, and had managed not only to graduate, but to make it all the way to college. An arts institute really. SAT scores not an entrance requirement.

He was an actor. Or was going to be an actor. Of course, he couldn't act and therefore suffered from unemployment for the rest of his life, but he looked like an actor, acted like an actor, and that is what we loved about him.

I think the first time I saw him in the Galleria, where we, the loners and lesser-knowns went to waste time, I fell in love. He smiled wide and open. A golden boy with blond curly hair and big white teeth. Fair and even-complected, his six-foot frame hung with the smooth tight flesh of his nineteen years.

Why he had come back to Portland that summer after my first semester at Jefferson, I am not sure, though I imagine it was so he could do the thing all small-town people do when they get out: come back to rub it in the naysayers' faces.

Brian and Anji had known each other at Jefferson prior to my transferring in. Been in the theater group there together, done *The Wiz* or some shit that bonded them for life. It had been *The Wiz*, and this one time when they were walking somewhere, and Brian had said to Anji, "Pull your dress up and show your snatch to the traffic," she had done it and laughed like hell.

I did not have to walk up to Brian that day in the Galleria. I couldn't have anyway—I was too shy, too retarded, I thought. And of course, though I was queer, I had not, at fifteen, honed the radar to locate another gay man in a crowd. He could have been straight. Or worse, laughing—not smiling—at me.

We saw each other one or two more times there during the next week and a half or so before he finally came up to me. I sat at one of the tables at the Coffee Ritz, where you could hold a space for hours on one fifty-cent cup of coffee. He was with Anji that day. I recognized her, though we did not nod or say anything to each other. She lagged behind as he stood above me.

"Hi, I'm Brian. You go to Jeff too?" Meaning "too" as in "in addition to Anji," who was applying some lipstick in the mirror of a hand-held compact over at their table.

"Yeah, I just transferred in last semester," I said.

"How do you like it?" he asked, then answered for me, "Sucks doesn't it?"

"*Portland* sucks," I said.

I saw a glow like a halo come off his blond hair. He was wearing shorts that showed the same golden hair on his legs. He sat down in the empty chair opposite me. "What do you do at Jeff?" Meaning, like, sports, etc., I guessed. I told him I played the cello. I was a part of the arts magnet program, though it slightly embarrassed me to admit it. It was an ungainly instrument, one I had to drag with much effort onto and off of school buses, and one for which I took a lot of ribbing. Brian did not tease me about it. Did not tease me that I, after a moment of noticing his interest, continued on with some fervor over my love for the music and the instrument.

"In most orchestras, it is all about the first violinist. I mean, everyone gets into the first violinist. You know, they get to come out last, and take a bow, and shake hands with the conductor, and stuff...but the cello adds depth in a way that a violin can't. Do you know what I mean?"

Brain nodded at me, looked in my eyes. I shifted my gaze down and continued. "I want to play in an orchestra one day. But don't think that's all I'm into. I really like the Go-Go's and A Flock of Seagulls, too."

Brian listened as I spoke. His foot touched mine and he did not draw it away as if it were a mistake to be undone.

When I finished with my story he told me about a concert that was happening that night, that he and Anji were going to go see Men Without Hats but they had to get the money to buy the tickets and were headed to the plasma center to trade marrow for cash. "Do you want to go too?" I wasn't sure if he meant the plasma center or the concert. Whichever, I said, "Yes." We went to the plasma center. Brian became my boyfriend.

The first time Brian and I made love, "Tainted Love" was playing on his stereo. I was aghast at the enormity of his penis and how, in comparison, mine seemed so small. I can't recall if he got hard, or if he came, though I think he did. I know that I did neither. Petrified, my dick stayed shrunken. I only knew cursory movements to perform.

Those I had seen in porno magazines. I suppose I acted them out just as if they were pictures to be flipped though. One frozen moment after another.

He did not comment on my style or lack of it. What I do remember clearly, though, is that after, we showered together and he hugged me in the warm water. Soaped my back and rubbed it. Kissed the back of my neck with his arms wrapped around my thin frame. He laughed kindly, opened my mouth with his. Called me by my name. Dried me with a towel. Watched attentively as I dressed. Held my hand. Brian was all I could see in any corner of the earth at any moment from then on, whether he was actually physically there or not.

After that summer, when Brian had to go back to California to attend school, Anji and I stayed friends. She supported my hacking huge chunks of hair out of my otherwise pretty black mop so I could look more war-torn, more suicidal, more Timothy Hutton in *Ordinary People*. I, of course, supported her lying down in the middle of busy intersections faking heart attacks.

It was Anji who told me about Brian's death. I don't know where he was when it happened or who she heard it from. The rumor was that he had left the arts institute or been asked to leave and moved to Japan where he had become a hustler. He had changed his name to something porno-y. He was the first to go from AIDS. The first I knew who got infected and fell. Anji and I closed ourselves inside a meat locker in the garage of her parents' house when we found out Brian was dead. Climbed in and shut the door. I think we less intended to kill ourselves through suffocation than wanted to feel what Brian felt right then. Dead, cold, alone.

Jonathan: Would you like it if I made you drink my piss?

Slave: Respectfully, Sir, I want whatever you want for me.

Jonathan: Can you take a full mouth of piss?

Slave: Yes, *SIR*. Make me your pisspig, *SIR.* Full mouth, *SIR*.

Jonathan: Can you hold all my piss in your mouth?

Slave: Yes, also drink it, *SIR*.

Jonathan: If you let even a drop of my piss fall out of your mouth, I am going to beat the shit out of you. Do you understand?

Slave: Yes, *SIR*. Nothing will be wasted, *SIR*.

Jonathan: You wouldn't spill any of my piss just to get me to lash you, would you?

Slave: Humiliate me, please, *SIR*.

Jonathan: You wouldn't play that game with me, would you?

Slave: No, *SIR.* I don't do that just to get you angry, *SIR.*

Jonathan: Because I won't be topped from the bottom. Do you understand?

Slave: Yes, *SIR.* I don't play those games, *SIR.*

Jonathan: Take off your clothes.

Slave: May I respectfully ask if the Master is going to take his clothes off too, Sir?

Jonathan: No, you may not ask. Take off your clothes.

Slave: Yes, *SIR.*

He remains on his hands and knees

looking up toward me as he slides his things off and pushes them to the side. I slip the belt out of the loops of my jeans and hand it to him.

Jonathan: Take this belt and tie it around your balls. Tie your balls off.

Slave: Tied, *SIR*.

Jonathan: Is it tied tight?

Slave: Yes, *SIR*.

Jonathan: Pull it tighter. I want you to pull it very tight so that your balls are shiny-tight. Do you understand?

Slave: Yes, *SIR*. Done, *SIR*.

Jonathan: I am going to gather up your balls and punch them if you look away from me.

Slave: Never, *SIR*.

I reach down and yank the belt that constrains his balls. They are purple now.

Jonathan: Please open your mouth.

Slave: Yes, *SIR*. Slavemouth open, *SIR*.

Jonathan: I am over you, is that clear?

There is a hesitation.

Slave: I got scared for a second, Sir.

Jonathan: Tell me why you were scared.

Slave: When you said you were over me, I thought you meant over as in done with, Sir. I didn't realize you were referring to your power over me at first, Sir.

Jonathan: Please open your mouth.

Slave: Yes, *SIR*. May I take your piss, *SIR*?

Jonathan: I want you for one second to close your eyes and imagine my piss in your mouth.

Slave: Yes, *SIR,* nice hot *MASTER* piss.

Jonathan: Can you imagine it in your mouth, slave? Running down your chest?

Slave: In my mouth, *SIR*. Never down my chest, *SIR*.

Jonathan: Why not down the chest?

Slave: I would not waste it, Sir.

I unzip the fly of my jeans and place my cockhead next to his open mouth. His eyes are closed, imagining, as I ordered, what my piss will feel like when it splashes his face. I have to concentrate for a moment to relax enough for the pee to come out. Finally it does. There is not much, but what there is, he drinks.

Jonathan: Do you like that pissboy?

Slave: Yes, *SIR*, love it *SIR*.

Jonathan: Is that what you are? A pissboy?

Slave: Worship it, *SIR*. *Your* pissboy, *SIR*. *Your* pissboy that loves and adores you, *SIR*.

Jonathan: You are a piss-whore.

Slave: I am *Your* pisswhore-bitch, *SIR*. I am *YOUR* faggottoiletslave, *SIR*.

Jonathan: I want to take you into the bathroom, piss-whore. I want you to crawl on your knees to the bath-room and blow me on the toilet.

Slave: Yes, *SIR*. Would be honored, *SIR*.

I walk to the bathroom which is very near where we are enacting this scene. He crawls behind me, naked, covered in slobber and piss. The lid of the toilet is flipped open already; I drop my pants and sit down. I repeat a litany of those words I know he likes best—cunt, whore, bitch—while he sucks my dick. I hold my dick at the base to make it harder than it would be naturally. To make it appear stiff, though it is not.

> *Jonathan:* Work the fucking spunk outta my nuts, piss-whore, while you jack your pisswhore dick.

After a moment the slave finally ejaculates, dumping his load onto the porcelain base of the toilet I am seated on. He pants and seems dis-oriented, no longer looking at me with his full attention.

> *Jonathan:* Lean in to me and put your ear near my mouth.

> *Slave:* Yes, *SIR*.

He leans in so that we are chest to chest. He cocks his head to the side so that his ear is nearly against my mouth and I whisper:

> *Jonathan:* You are disgusting

and I hate you.

Slave: Yes, Sir.

Anji and I neither touched nor spoke nor cried in the meat locker that day. We were just there, together, until we could no longer take it, or believed our homage to Brian was complete. Later that night, Anji's sister, Rica, who knew Brian as well and who was at that time a dancer of the modern variety, danced in a white dress on the lawn in the backyard of Anji's parents' house, the sprinkler system fully blowing and drenching her. We sat, still chilled from the freezer, as Rica repeatedly threw herself to the ground in some Graham-ish contractions and spun enough so that the grass was ripped up by the force. Eventually, when she was soaked through and smeared with mud, Rica completed her dance with a mock death. We did not clap. It was not that kind of performance.

Dear J—

I read something about you in a local rag. I knew you would eventually get your name from there to here. It was a local-boy puff-piece with a picture of you. Nice, but you know, stupid too. I sent the picture along (shake out the envelope).

Remember Pamela Webber from Jefferson? Frizzy-haired cheerleader bitch? She is the new anchorwoman for that television news magazine show, Hollywood Action!

Cutthroat. She must fuck like a demon. Her hair is too gruesome to allow her fame but she got it. Tight pussy. That's what I think. Also ran into your cousin, Denise. She was wondering if you were dead since she hasn't heard from you in so long. I'll spread the rumor that you are. It'll generate interest.

XO
—A.

P.S. Stay w/ the bad therapist. They all suck and just want your money anyway so why switch? Besides, Jonathan, who needs more misery?

I have a "mail to" tag on my webpage. It is an outright beg for praise for having had the brains to figure out HTML, but it is also in hopes that I will receive hate mail. It was my intention, when putting up the pages, to offend as many people as possible with the material I have made available.

I don't have a "you must be 18 to view this material" warning on my pages. What I do have is fist-fuckers, ball-torturers, and shit-eaters. My pages are picture intensive, though I have done what I can to make them fast-loading. I want to catch a looker before he gets too bored to wait for the complete image to unravel. If you are sitting in front of your computer with a hard-on, forty seconds can be a long time to wait for a 30k image of a man stuffing his hand up his own ass.

As you scroll though the pages they progressively depict graphic, more graphic, and very graphic sexual images. Especially on the shit-eater page. I know there are people who really dig on shit. And I am not trying to bust on them. But I'm not one and I have never really met a shit aficionado, or at least not one willing to tell me they were except through the "mail to" tag that I have on that particular page, which I named "The Shit Gallery."

I look at shock as armor in a life that is essentially one brutal offensive strike. Shock covers up my actually being a prude and also really sensitive in a totally dangerous, volatile way. Gag them before they can gag you, before they can get to know you. If they stay around after the initial assault, there is promise. I practice this philosophy in life as well as on the Internet.

I have dated some nice men. One in particular. An attorney. Very clean, from a clean family. He did not cheat, did some humanistic-style *pro bono* work (you know, for welfare gays, etc.). He was young, handsome, and physically fit, yet a cigarette smoker, which is good.

I wanted to love him even though he fucked like an attorney. Aggression, aggression, aggression. I thought maybe we could meet somewhere between my past and his ironed sheets. I had hope, until he told me about his family. A happy story. So much love. Also stories of the happiest time of his life: high school. We never had another date after that night.

It's not like I have to have someone who is miserable, though depression can be hot in a glam, suicide-threat sort of way. But I knew he clearly would not survive a second round of even the cleanest version of my life history. Maybe I sold him short, but I don't think so. I mean, he smokes light cigarettes, which is really pussy (and embarrassing in public).

Today I got eighteen emails from shit fans. Some wondered why I didn't have any piss-drinkers or animal-fuckers. Shit-eaters are greedy. In some of the emails are requests to meet. I guess they are thrilled someone has made a publicly accessible shrine to crap, but also because they think I am a fox. One of the pages entitled "Lewd Homosexual Photos of Your Host," has three non-cock, -ball or -butthole photos of me from my time as a Porno Prince (not King or Star). I want them to see my face. I want them to see in my photos that, despite my heavily tattooed arms, shaved head, my attempt to comply with the photographer's wish that I make sexy sex faces, I am in fact a boy, not a man, and I am not far from a final, deadly heroin nod.

That is the part of my life that men like the light-cigarette-smoking attorney could never get their minds around. The sex-industry part. They inevitably disappoint me by wanting to hear the stories. Tell me about the weirdest one. Tell me about the hottest one, ugliest dick, biggest nipple, oldest, youngest. Light-cigarette smokers never ask me to tell them how I ignored customers even though they were paying huge sums of money, or how they usually left totally unsatisfied and hating me. Truth ruins fantasy.

Sex is sexy but sometimes it is fucked too. So far, no one has really gotten the juxtaposition of the "galleries" of photos played against my miserable face, with the exception of one guy. He commented that he thought I was a performer. That these pages were my show. He asked me if I was a performance artist. What the hell is a performance artist? Someone who is neither performer nor artist but, rather, some lazy, sloppy, mish-mash of an angry Upper East Sider in a Lower East Side venue. "Eat some shit": now *that's* a show in my book.

I went and saw a dance recital at the Joyce Theater about a year ago. It was a Butoh-meets–East Village thing. *Huh?* Right. Well, that is how they actually advertised it. I would never have gone but the ticket was free, and I thought I could at least boo, and that would be fun.

As I knew it would, the whole thing stank. It was amateurish and convoluted. Lots of the same arm movements that are gestures we all do everyday without the huge, noisy, and completely unnecessary dancerish exhalation accompanying them. There were some girls with butts big enough to keep them out of a ballet company rolling on the ground, and one Asian guy, who I guess was the Butoh one, making faces and curling his fingers up like tree branches on *The Wizard of Oz* evil forest trees.

Those tickets were seventeen dollars each, but we were way up and on the side. It turned out those seats could not have been better. I thought I heard a burp. It made me giggle. I figured someone else was so beyond bored they couldn't even bother to muffle their gas. I looked down to where the sound came from just in time to see a blonde woman lean forward and spray huge amounts of puke onto the people in front of her. I clapped and then, you know, left. The show was over. She was not a performance artist, though her performance merited the seventeen dollars twice over. Because it wasn't a contrivance of something real and interesting; it was real.

Not to say my pages on the Internet are all that interesting. What I am saying is my pages are real in the puke-lady-at-the–Joyce Theater way. If you need me well scrubbed, trussed, tight, smiling, and ready to eat your shit, you can't have me. Because while some Asian guy may get up there in whiteface and twist his hands around in some bubble of conceptual lighting for you, the truly interesting show is happening somewhere else, played out in the darkest, hardest-to-see, and most uncomfortable part of the theater, for free.

PISS BOTTLE

This morning when I woke up, I smelled something. Nothing like a burning car tire, or spoiled meat, but just something.

It was a faint olfactory on-switch which behaved in the way perfume on a woman is meant to. This provocative ghost of a scent passing on air arousing some shadowy memory. Yet this was not quite that. Shadowy, yes; provocative, no.

First, of course, there is always the reasoning away of what the stink is not. Not the stink of too many cigarettes smoked. Not the moldering cloud from the pile of cum-hardened socks mounting next to the computer. And then I knew. It was the days-old ripening of my piss bottle.

I remember the first time I used a piss bottle. It was probably drug related. Too high to care to go to the toilet. Too apathetic to worry that a Sprite bottle of warm piss might be an alarming sign that I had given up on even the most basic characteristics of personal care. I mean, I meant to do it just that once. Yet, it has since become a habit.

For the most part, I use a piss bottle when I am involved with something whose attention requires I not break whatever trance I've fallen into, like when watching *Charmed* on the WB network. A time when I find a trip to the bathroom can have the startling effect of awakening me from my unreality stupor and drawing me away from the plot reveal.

Yet sometimes now, at its most awful, I can have as many as five full-up piss bottles. I guess I watch a lot of meaningful TV. Sadly. However, I've grown accustomed to them and take care to keep their inventory in check with rules. No piss bottles on the floor to avoid a kick-over, plus a candy wrapper stuffed in the neck of each to identify they aren't for drinking any longer.

Then there was the day I went from a piss bottle, to a piss glass; I did have a moment's worry about what it meant that I was willing to fill the cups I take life-sustaining water from with yellow waste. Would my pee alter the condition of that cup forever? Once a demitasse, forever a Port-o-San. Would I, in time, no longer be able to say definitively which glasses, mugs, and cups had been piss glasses and which had not? No, I would not. No, I cannot. And so, what of it?

On a handful of occasions when my lonely, obsessive, and time-consuming masturbation has pushed ordinary limits, I've drunk my own urine straight from my penis. Yet cold pee in a glass is dirty? It doesn't make sense, though I do sort of feel it does. Maybe it has something to do with freshness.

Hot pee sprayed directly from my dick cooked at an internal temperature of 98.6

degrees just seems okay to me. Cold pee, left to the open air, forms this strange translucent layer, like an accidentally boiled potato leek soup does or like hot cocoa always seems to. Not that I am drinking my cold pee, but I do leave it to stand, and I know a scum ring when I see one and know it's not good.

Forty feet. What is that for me? Twenty-two steps from the farthest point in my apartment to the toilet, and I just can't seem to make it there much of the time.

Maybe if I had a social life I would do the things people who have to face other people do, like pee in a toilet. But to improve a rigor-mortis corpse of a social life requires doing things I so deeply abhor. Going to cocktail parties and business-card-passing PR mixers. I mean, hey, I could force myself to attend the parties I am invited to, but what then? Listen to pashmina-wearing Condé Nast anorectic whippets prattle on in cocaine-fueled marketing blurbs about how fantastic their lives are? Guzzle booze in a continuous and dangerous binge so I can bear to disclose to people the truth about myself in return? "You're the attorney with a medical degree, the face for Chloé, the editrix for *I'm Hot Shit and You Aren't* magazine, and you're only sixteen? Cool." "Oh, me? My house is littered with piss-filled soda bottles."

Anyway—after having awakened this morning to that smell, I really might need to readjust my thinking in terms of what is passable in terms of urine receptacles. Luck can only hold out so long. And that being true, ultimately (if the stink alone isn't enough to get me to halt the carefree flow) the odds are in favor that one day soon I will accidentally drink from a piss bottle, kick one over, or worse, accidentally serve a full one to you. Cocktail anyone?

CITIZEN OF CHAOS

It was at a memorial service tonight that I was again brought into a conversation about chaos. It was something I'd recently been asked my opinion on in completely unrelated circumstances. During that first conversation, afraid I would seem unstable, I hesitantly shared my opinion. The Universe, I said, is horribly aggressive and constantly in the process of chipping away at us. In small bits or large chunks chaos will consume us whole, then blow us apart for no reason other than it can or possibly, it must. Luckily he, the other person involved in the chat, concurred. As a scientist he reasoned that the look of stability in the Universe, of order, is sheer trickery. That ultimately, all laws are mutable beyond even the most seemingly complete reasoning out.

I did not always imagine the Universe this way. Though I think the lack of a notion about chaos came simply from the naïve acceptance of my parent's rule that we are part of a perfect plan driven by the divine. A plan where the blackest nature of human deeds are explained as a part of some puzzle whose pieces can only be viewed in entirety by God.

Then, in 1990, during my first year of college, my first year away from home, I was speeding along McBean Parkway toward downtown Los Angeles in the passenger seat of a VW driven by a boy named Manjit. I remember the speed at which we were traveling; that is was clear and warm; and that he, Manjit, was extremely beautiful. In a moment, my head was out the window. Hair pushed back flat, my mouth open, taking in the air that beat my face. And then, it came up out of me. Organic and ready: "I renounce Jesus as my personal Savior." I felt ebullient. I said it again, louder, yelling not with anger but abandon. "I renounce Jesus Christ as my personal Savior." Manjit laughed the open laugh of a young man. And I felt free, not so much free from the "oppressive patriarchal church" as from the conventions of my upbringing. I was less denouncing Christ than I was accepting that I was an adult free to choose paths and ideas beyond those I had simply absorbed through repetitive experience.

It was a thrilling moment, one I still recall with joy; yet, had I known then what I know now, that it was not my first day as a free person but my last, I would have it undone. My acceptance and unquestioned belief in God or Christ, a belief in a divine force, had kept me from facing the power of the Universe as anything other than ordered or manipulated for the ultimate goodness of my life. In renouncing Christ and God, and their subtle power as psychological, ideological underpinning, I shed faith from my existence and replaced it with chance. I had opened my eyes to a new philosophy, or rather, shut them to former constructs, only to find I was now a citizen of chaos, a more furious jailer than any cage of uninspected beliefs.

In the conversation I had tonight, I again put forward my thesis, then did my best to follow the disputation of the person standing before me. She spoke of her spiritually defining moments experienced through the use of acid. Told me of the understanding she came to have of the greatness of the Universe and our role in it. "We have to think of our lives as theater," she stated, "and the Universe is sort of like the director. The director won't be mad at us if we just know our role really well and that maybe our role sometimes must unexpectedly change. But we must act, continue to act." I started to focus on her jewelry, wondered why she chose to wear her hair as she did. Wondered her age. Looked for signs of lines or bags beneath her eyes. Nodded. Smiled. I, wondering of a Universe composed from an LSD trip, wondered was that sound enough to count or was it pitiable. I concluded that while it seemed enough for her, it was weak and stupid to this outsider.

There was another person there during the conversation at the memorial service. He laughed when I stated my opinion and patted my leg. He mothered my fatalism as a passing fancy then, after the LSD lady was through, shared his sage experience. "We cannot fight it," he said, meaning chaos, "so instead we must toss ourselves into it and take of the ride what we can." It was reassuring for a moment. Laissez-faire. Why not? Don't curse a fate we cannot control; just forget about it. I could almost have accepted it had he not, later, cornered me near the "guest book" table, leaned his body into mine, rose to his tiptoes, and attempted to stick his tongue in my mouth. A tongue I didn't want. His disreputable behavior made him more chaos' henchman than a surfer on its tide.

I walked away from that man and from the entire conversation. At a memorial service you can't bitch-slap a masher nor dispute chaos to dust. There is no need. That we were gathered to remember the life of a person who suffered cancer so aggressive it ate her vital organs to jelly, killing her at fifty, spoke for me. She, the dead, was silently testifying to my belief: you cannot protect yourself from the force of man or nature, but rather must rend, mold, and cast as best you can the forms you need to serve your purpose before the random knocks you to the floor or closes your eyes forever.

This is what I know for fact: I get hungry when I don't want to be hungry. As often as not things go wrong when I need them to go right. A desire or hope for some great event is likely met with emptiness and regret at those hopes having not borne fruit. That I am powerless to make anything that cannot be destroyed by other people or forces that are also careening on an unchartable path set in motion by the breath of pandemonium that is our Universe.

And while I feel strongly that I am right, I wouldn't mind being disproved. Though I think a reversal would take something extraordinary, something I cannot seem to attain. Something no hippie or french-kissing queen has been able to inspire or reignite in me: faith. A letting go, a trust that

I will not be consumed before my time if I rested from battling and hating the Universe for its refusal to be controlled. I do not want the cancer to get me. Though in some way, sometimes, I think living with my understanding of chaos, trying to make reason of an unordered world, living without some god, any god, to blame, can be a horrible and destructive cancer of its own.

R.K.

I don't know what has been wrong with me lately. Everything has this weird ectoplasm around it that keeps me from being able to see straight. I guess what is wrong with me lately is that I am really alone.

Part of that is that my friends have somehow gotten the money to go places that I have not. It is empty here in general over the summer weekends, but in my apartment, specifically, it is very quiet. No phone ringing and just that damned Labor Day weekend *Twilight Zone* marathon on the television. *Twilight Zone*, jack off, *Twilight Zone*, jack off. That is about all I have come up with so far to keep myself entertained.

I start to make long-distance phone calls when I am feeling like this. I called my one friend, Annie, and she actually picked up the phone crying. I was so happy, of course, because that meant, one: that we could talk about her and not me, and two: that she was as fucked up as me. Her misery was due to ovulation, I was to discover, but still she was miserable, chemical or not, and there was solace in that.

I talked to her about how I had been hiring all these hustlers to keep me company and how it is generally okay, except financially, of course. And how I made the huge mistake of having a real, free trick come over and how after, he wanted to hug and talk. I just wanted to say you can stay if you don't touch me, or talk to me, or insist that you get to sleep in my bed with me. Of course, proper postcoital conduct disallows this, so I just put on my pants and said something like, "Wanna shower before you go?"

There is someone else I always try to reach when New York is empty and I am feeling like shit. He was my lover for six years who eventually left me for another man. Because of this I think he owes it to me to listen to me complain, and he usually will, if I can ever get a hold of him. He moves more often than I do, and that is a lot. It always ends up being worth the effort to locate him and worth the cost of the toll call because, even though he left me, he inevitably says the one thing I want to hear most in the whole world: "It was a huge mistake to leave you."

I think his relationship with the other guy is good, so he is not saying it to degrade his lover; rather, it's probably because after he left me he went blind. I can tell he thinks that, had he stayed with me, his sight would not have been stolen. I used to burn a lot of candles when we were together.

My dumpers always end up pretty bad. One is now dead of AIDS, two are sick with AIDS, one fell off a bridge and drowned, and then there's Richard, the blind one. I like to think about that sometimes and remember that while I may be lonely, my face isn't rotting off at the bottom of some river. It is all about degrees of feeling good and bad.

As far as men go now, I think I would like to get into another relationship; I actually have a date tomorrow night. I am hoping this one will evolve into something nice, though that hope alone usually destroys it before it can happen. Like when you go, "I want you to meet so-and-so. You guys are going to love each other," and then they don't love each other and even sometimes hate each other and subsequently hate you, too.

But this is a guy I have seen for years. At the gym, on the street. He is beautiful and all that, but what I really like about him is that he always seems very quiet and focused. He rarely tried to look up my shorts as I lay flat on a weight bench and he never got a hard-on in the shower like me and all the other guys. No one I know knows anything about him except his first name and that he is perfect in a gay way, meaning no one has heard any dirt on him.

I never thought to ask him out before because I smoke and he has a nonsmoker's body. He couldn't poison himself that way. Also, there is lots of dirt on me, and even perfect people, like him, like to get the scoop and make judgments.

Then I was walking my dog (who had just come home from the pet hospital where he receives dialysis, so I had something to talk about), and I saw him on the street. Thankfully it was one of the rare occasions I was not smoking as I walked and also not wearing stinking filthy clothes. I told him about the dog so he would think I was a really good soul, not the type to intentionally blind ex-boyfriends with my evil will.

I got a boner talking to him and I thought to hide it, but then I thought, why? I mean—I am a man, he is a man. We have penises and we like other men's penises. So here is mine. I am not saying I pushed my butt under so that it would stick out further, just that I did not cover it. Anyway, I walked the dog with him as he made his way home, and we made a date to talk on the phone to make a date to meet in real life sometime later.

Because I had been bumming all day, I was afraid he'd call at the point at which I was about to drive glass into my eyes and then I'd have to explain, and that never works unless the other person is about to drive glass into their eyes too. But my ovulating friend Annie said just do this, just do that, and I was like, "Okay." And it was over.

The perfect man called just then. I could not have been happier or planned it better. We talked for a while about books and CDs. Made fun of in-line skaters and the Roxy disco clones. He told me some about his family, and I got that he wasn't absolutely perfect—though the fact that he admitted he is white trash brings him pretty close in my book. I was relieved. I wished that he was there with me so I could have shown him that, under the right circumstances, I don't have to wish people blind.

I guess I will have my chance when we go out to eat tomorrow. For now, I am thinking of his body in that shower, his dick not hard, not a pig, and thrilled that, unlike most of the men I have been with in recent times, I get to discover his dick later.

HALLOWEEN
1978

I want the biggest pumpkin I can find at the pumpkin patch. I want to spend the day running through the fields. Seeing the faces in my mind that I will eventually cut into the pumpkin. Mom is wearing a sweater and some funny rubber boots. She has a hat on her head made from green wool that looks beautiful with her red hair. Dad has some of those rubber boots on too, though they are black, not yellow like Mom's. His brown bell-bottom cords, worn smooth on the thigh, are tucked into the tops of his boots. When he smiles I can see his black tooth, though I don't think it is gross. I just think it is Dad. Anne, my sister, is heavy. She has to take steroids for asthma. After we get home the whole family goes to the kitchen to carve and clean out the innards. Sometimes we put one of the jack-o'-lanterns on the porch on top of a big stool and drape a long coat around it and put some shoes beneath the coat with the tips sticking out so it looks like a person sitting there! I am going trick-or-treating as a pirate and Anne is going as a flapper.

1984

I was going to go trick-or-treating with Wendall and some other guys that are in my class. We figured this was the last time we could go out since we'll be in the 7th grade next year. We talked a lot about how much candy we want to get and how, if we couldn't get as much as we wanted, then we would hide in the bushes by Wendall's house and steal some from other kids. Probably I am not going now, though, because when Wendall started calling me a fag at school everyone started calling me it. Jeannie asked me if John Travolta was my boyfriend and I didn't even know what to say. Wendall was the one who wanted to fool around. He told me he wanted to show me what his brothers did to each other and he showed me how to suck his dick and he tried to put his dick in my butt. So he told everyone that I tried to rape him, which is not how it was, but they all believed him anyway.

1995

I wanted to get that red kind of heroin, Red Devil, or whatever it is called. The kind that all the rock stars are overdosing on. But I don't know where to get it. I am not a rock star. And even if I were, I probably wouldn't go out tonight. Halloween belongs to the borough kids. There is something, a horror movie, on TV. I like the aggressive poltergeist-y ones best. Where the spirits take over a family or destroy a house and no one knows what is going on, just that everything got ruined. I have some regular white heroin anyway.

THANKSGIVING
1978

I think Bob and Betsey are coming over. We call them cousins though they really aren't blood relatives. We have just known them a long time. Betsey always makes the best desserts. I think she is a real chef. Once she was an archaeologist but she wasn't able to dig up anything good so she quit. Bob is a foot doctor. I don't like to shake his hand. I know later that I will be able to drink some Cold Duck though it will have a little bit of water mixed in. My mom says in Italy all the kids get to drink wine 'cause that is their culture. Some of my most favorite foods are being made by Mom. Brussels sprouts with chestnuts mixed in. Baby carrots with brown sugar mixed in, then a huge turkey. Is this the holiday they play *The Wizard of Oz* or is that Easter? I don't even think there are any *Charlie Brown*s for Thanksgiving, but pretty soon that one about the really small, sad Christmas tree will be on. I like that one 'cause even sad trees get some love and that is a good story.

1984

Mom is quiet today; she is quiet a lot. Since she said she is going to run away and never come back, she doesn't talk much. I see her reading the Bible. When I tell her about something that is bothering me, she quotes from it. She isn't really cooking food for tonight, but there is a turkey in the oven. We all sit around and are quiet until is it ready. I guess it is just turkey tonight and nothing else, which is okay. Then Mom goes to pull the turkey out. It slips from her hands and falls onto the floor. It splits open at the breast. There is a greasy pool underneath it that is spreading slowly. Mom takes the pot holders off her hands, puts them down on the stove, and walks into the den. She sits down and starts to read the Bible. We all, my sister and me, just look at the turkey on the floor and then sort of walk out of the kitchen. Anne leaves the house and I go to my bedroom.

1995

This girl I went to school with works in a

Chinese restaurant. Even though we have never hung out, sometimes she will steal a bag of fortune cookies for me. She knows I am broke a lot and they fill me up for free. I have some peanut butter to smear on the fortune cookies. When I call my mom to wish her a happy Thanksgiving, I call late. I crunch a peanutty fortune cookie into the phone and tell her it is left-over pecan pie one of my friends made me to take home after a really great dinner. She believes it. It makes her happy to believe things are good, or maybe too sad to catch me in a lie. They still haven't made a *Charlie Brown* for Thanksgiving.

CHRISTMAS
1978

Mom and Dad and Anne and me are going to go to a tree farm today and get the perfect tree. I always say I want one that is at least eleven feet tall. I know it won't fit in the house, but if I say I want a smaller one then I bet we wouldn't even get a six-foot tree. When we get to the tree farm, there is a horse ride on a flatbed that has hay all over it. You can look for good trees from the back of it while you are pulled through the woods, though really you have to go way inside the woods to find the special one meant just for you.

1984

Mom put a small tree in a pot on top of a table in the den. There are some ornaments on it but no lights. It is hard to string lights and I think Mom is too tired to go through that. I haven't told her what I want for Christmas this year 'cause probably, like the last few years, there isn't going to be anything. Not even something I don't want. My sister, Anne, might get me something. She buys me and her shampoo and soap and toilet paper when we need it. She is working at a restaurant now. My mom had to sign something to make it okay for her to work because she's fourteen, and I think you have to be sixteen to really work. I guess she likes the job. Sometimes I visit her there and she lets me eat anything I want. Sometimes she brings food home because Mom can forget to buy any. Anne might buy me some underwear, which is what I really want. It is hard to go to gym class and have to change with all those guys and not have any good underwear. I'm not going to ask her though, because at Christmas you are supposed to get what you really want just by wanting it extra hard. That is the magic of Christmas.

1995

I have been playing the Carpenters' Christmas tape all morning. Karen Carpenter has a voice like an angel. Sometimes I think I would like to spend Christmas with someone, but it is easier not to. I finish the bottle of Frangelico liqueur a tenant who lives in one of the buildings I super gave me. I don't think liquor stores are open on Christmas. I am going to go to bed. It's still early but it gets dark early now. Very dark.

SUPERSTAR

I love candy, especially chocolaty-flavored Ex-Lax. It tastes so good and has a quick turnaround time. I like regular candy too, but it is not so easily disposed of and that vomit-inducing liquid-charcoal syrup of Ipecac isn't available over the counter. I could probably find a doctor willing to exchange sex for the prescription, but I don't think he would want me showing up for the date with teeth made loose and rotten by a constant stream of acidic stomach bile.

I got the idea for the chocolaty Ex-Lax after watching *Superstar: The Karen Carpenter Story* by Todd Haynes. You know the one. It is all done with Barbie dolls and voiceovers. I like especially when they carve away the Karen doll's face to make her look real thin. The friend who I watched the movie with thinks there is something wrong with me that the message I took away from the film was that chocolaty Ex-Lax is slimming and not that obsessive dieting can kill even a superstar.

When Olestra came out on the market, I was fortunate enough to get my hands on some of the potato ships made with the new fat substitute. Everyone was so concerned about the possibility of negative side effects from Olestra. It seems that Olestra punishes the piggy snacker with the onslaught of debilitating nausea and diarrhea, which keeps you from eating more so you lose weight you never even gained from the chips in the first place. Negative calorie intake. Duh, *perfect,* but too gross-tasting to eat at every meal.

Currently I am taking one over-the-counter diet pill a day. A sixteen-hour appetite suppressant. The packaging is oddly shaped. It is in the family of penis-shaped lipsticks, or some other genital-familiar product. In and of itself, the product is not about sex, at least not blatantly, but it makes you feel sexier. I think it was Soft & Dri Baby Powder deodorant that was shaped *just* like a cock. With a huge head and all. The message being: if you want to get a man, or at least his organ, don't smell like you.

There are more penis-shaped beauty items than vagina-shaped, however the diet pills I am currently taking come in a flat packet that resembles a picture of a uterus from a high school sex-ed poster. Many women, many I know, hate what they refer to as their "pussy bulge"—that area below the bellybutton and above the pubis. It is likely that the package is intended to send some sort of subliminal message that these pills are specifically manufactured to take that "pussy bulge" to flatness, or that the pill will otherwise attack that area in some way. I haven't seen a diet-pill package shaped like a butt or a thigh, but that doesn't mean it doesn't exist.

Getting near the end of my diet-aid solutions, I have gone to a plastic surgeon. She said she could not, in good conscience, do facial- or body-resculpturing (liposuction) for me, though she was willing to pin my ears, shave my chin, staple my stomach, and make my lips so big it would create the same overall effect of thinness I am striving for. The last time I had collagen injections they lasted only about two weeks. For five hundred dollars, I thought this was kind of a rip-off. This kid I know got some illegal permanent lip implants in Mexico. Probably they are cancer-causing like many breast implants have been suspected of being, though I believe it is a risk many are willing to take. Myself included.

The first plastic surgery I had was in the late '80s. I was still a teenager. It was not a planned event, but rather the result of a face-pulverizing motorcycle accident. I remember crying when I took the bandages off in my bathroom three weeks before I was supposed to. I neither recognized nor liked the new face. I think my lover at the time was also pretty unnerved, though rather than explain what he was feeling, while in a deep sleep, he would just punch my face over and over.

It was not that the face I was given as a result of the reconstruction was bad. I did not end up looking monstrous. It was just different—very different. It was hard to pinpoint the exact change. Yes, the nose was bigger before, but more than that there had been an overall transformation.

Sometimes I feel the person I was before is still under the face I carry now. Like phantom-limb syndrome. And the face I have now belies the life and experiences I had prior to the accident.

When I tell people this, it is rare that they grasp what I am saying or understand in any way what it was like for me growing up ugly and then being reborn, in a way, an entirely different creature. What I mean is—my postoperative face is *better*. Better than before and actually better than most. Sleek and aquiline. There are cheekbones where there were none before, the mouth a surgeon's textbook model. One day I was fat and geeky, the butt of jokes and always the scapegoat. The next I was not. It was not about me, about anyone loving me more, but about my skin being made more loveable.

Despite having been made "better," I never walk with my head up. In fact, I most often wear a baseball cap to avoid eye contact. The wanton looks of other available men continue to disturb me. I know they want the face and I know they want the body and I know too that they would not want the insides if I ever let them see them, because inside I still live the life of an ugly, fat teen. Men don't like that dichotomy. They want a charmed face to belong to a charmed man. And I am hardly that.

It is hard for me to let go of the thought that, had I not undergone a catastrophic physical change during a period of life when each of us is most unsure and vulnerable about who we are, I would not suffer this mania and misery. I might be able to look up, to not be lonely, or angry. If my physical evolution had not been mashed by a car, that I would feel whole. I am still young. Perhaps my two selves will meld together in time. Though for today, I will just take another diet pill and even some oral steroids but no more chocolaty Ex-Lax. Because even superstars can overdose on Ex-Lax and I am, despite my Steve Austin experience, just plain ugly old me.

LIFE IN PASSING

Sitting here, waiting for my 32nd birthday to strike, I experience a reminiscence of feeling. A poke in the belly and a rapid fleeting image. Passing, perhaps, but replicating exactly my thoughts of seventeen years ago.

Seventeen years ago, when I thought I would never overcome the misery, never amount to anything, imagined there to be no way of ridding myself of the unmet and torturous wants. In that flash of memory a moment ago, in that split hair of a second: the gun, the pills, the note. A rope? The end.

What had I expected? Not this really. I had not expected, when at fifteen I decided suicide was dumb, that this was what I was sparing the blade for. An apartment that crumbles at the corners and leaks outside air. An income pieced together through varied and most often miserable means. I had not expected at thirty-two that I would have to suck power from the hallway of my building through an elaborate network of extension cords to supply myself with light. I did not expect to be alone. I did not expect I would alternately have diarrhea or be constipated.

I remember being seven. I don't know where we were. Some beach-type place. There was ice cream and cotton candy. Hundreds of tourists and as many gift stores. Wanting something to commemorate our grand vacation we (me and my family) made our way into a T-shirt shop. This was in the day when you could get iron-on. Good iron-on. Like it came from the manufacturer—not a Woolworth home appliqué kit.

I wanted my T-shirt to say STAR. Gold sparkle letters on black cotton. The shop guy asked if that was with two *R*s. I understood what he meant and I said no. "It is not a name—it is a *title.*" I imagined even at seven that something was supposed to happen, that I was special, that I was a star.

I was wrong.

I keep trying to remember that "STAR" T-shirt and trying to tap into that innocent trust in a magnificent future, but I can't anymore. Recently, someone asked me: if I could do it all over again, would I do it any differently? I hear this question asked frequently on talk shows. A question posed to those so great that a televised hour has been dedicated to their life. I have never heard one respondent answer yes. And it is no wonder. Why regret a life that has amounted to something? Success satisfactorily diminishes the failures of the past.

I answered yes, however. My response was not being shaped by an audience or a camera crew or a professional journalistic interrogator. I did not have to answer, "Nope—would not change a thing." I did not have to pretend that all life is a grand lesson, did not have to downplay the shit in order to make those whose lives are shittier nod their heads and feel better about the messes they have lived through. Would I change anything? Yes, yes I would. I would not be gay.

Sometimes when I am feeling particularly political or, at the very least, not depressed, I can say that being gay has taught me to be tough, to survive, to move beyond prejudice. It has allowed me to be in touch with my sensitive nature and my artistic side without apology. And that sounds good, but in the final analysis, I would chuck those subjective and lazy excuses for the simple feeling of belonging to the greater group. For the comfort and security of a stale day-to-day job only straight people seem to be able to hack over the long term. To let my gut get a little soft without negative sexual and social ramifications. To marry and not fear pussy. To back slap and har-har. To belong to a fraternity. To take a shower at the gym without having my cock stared at or moved on.

If I were straight I would not have to spend my life trying to *pass* as straight. I would not have needed to study the movements and rituals of heterosexual men so that I might successfully mimic them. Would not pay attention to my walk and my wrists and my demeanor. Would not dissect every consonant and vowel I speak to ensure the aspirated "th" or sibilant "s" are not apparent. It is agonizing. Yet, when I work extra-hard at passing, it is amazing the ease with which I move through the world, the access I am allowed. Simple things. Getting keys made. We men know what it is like to grind metal! Yeah. Whoo. Buying a sandwich. Extra cheese? You bet! No charge. Waiting for a subway train. "He's a homie—we won't mash him." Thanks.

"Internalized homophobia" is the rap-across-the-knuckles term coined to describe self-hating gays. I guess I suffer from that. That is my truth. However, I am not so dumb as to think I can join some Christian redo organization and have enough Jesus beat into me so that I can convert to heterosexuality. I don't believe in shock therapy, aversion therapy, drug therapy, or any other form of treatment for homosexuality. There isn't one. It isn't a disease, though I have allowed it to disease my life. That is just the way it is.

Thirty-two. I will be thirty-two on Sunday. No biggie in the greater scheme of things, I guess. I am a baby to my grandmother and aged to an eighth grader. But it is not the life I wanted. Unfortunately, exhaustively spending energy to simply survive being gay has kept what I wanted a mystery. I never took a moment to focus beyond honing skills that would help me not be hated. I just have taken step after step toward nothing. Just waiting for the sun to come up so I could get out of bed and do more of nothing, more getting by, more filling time until the sun sets. Getting by and passing as straight. I have wasted my life.

I don't want to be turning forty-two and still be mulling these same things over. I am scared that I will be. But I am more challenged by trying to direct myself toward a goal than by any other challenge I face. I don't know what a goal looks like. I have become afraid of goals, afraid that if I shoot for one it will be the wrong one, and I am running out of time. And, moreover, I fear that by meeting a goal, I must also meet myself. That pushing onward, forward, in an attempt to reach a prize requires inquiry into personal strength and a release of personal weakness. I am not hale and hearty—I am not well met. I am a coward. I have lost out on life, and for what? To pass as straight so I am not hated by others, so that I could end up, days before my birthday, hating myself.

Would I change anything? I guess if I think about it, I would still answer yes, but not "Yes, I wouldn't be gay." If given the chance, I would not have cared so much that I was. I would not have allowed it to matter that others did not like what I was. It is a dumb question though. The past cannot be changed. I can only try to forget it. To not think, in these transient moments, of the gun, the pill, the note. A rope? The end.

Thomas Woolley was born and raised on the West Coast where he attended the California Institute of the Arts in Los Angeles. It was here that he first practiced creative writing under the tutelage of a very sexy professor with whom he almost had an affair ten years later. He currently works in Manhattan at a national magazine in the marketing department where he is afforded the opportunity to create a lot of material dotted with excessive exclamation points. He lives in the much-maligned state of New Jersey with his lover and a cat so ferocious it had to be declawed.